MW01110306

1445

MA

Basketball

Bernie Blackall

Special thanks to Steve Buchanan,
Basketball Coach and Physical Educator,
Keeth Elementary School, for his
assistance during the production
of this book.

Heinemann
Interactive Library

Des Plaines,
Illinois

Acknowledgements

The publisher would like to thank the following for their kind assistance:
Rebel Sport, in Prahran
Students from: Armadale Primary School—Robert Klein, Nicola Murdock,
Khoa Nguyen, Mimosa Rizzo, Andrew Scott, Charlotte Sheck-Shaw, Zheng Yu;
Midway Elementary School—Whitney Tossie and Greg Tossie;
Keeth Elementary School—Alida Perez

© 1998 Reed Educational & Professional Publishing
Published by Heinemann Interactive Library,
an imprint of Reed Educational & Professional Publishing,
1350 East Touhy Avenue, Suite 240 West
Des Plaines, IL 60018

Every effort has been made to contact copyright holders of any material reproduced
in this book. Any omissions will be rectified in subsequent printings if notice is
given to the publisher.

The author and publishers are grateful to the following for permission to reproduce
copyright photographs: page 6 Ben Van Hook/Sports Illustrated; page 7 Manny Millan/Sports Illustrated

Designed by Karen Young
Edited by Angelique Campbell-Muir
Photography by Malcolm Cross
Illustrations by Vasja Koman
Production by Alexandra Tannock
Printed in Malaysia by Times Offset (M) Sdn. Bhd.

02 01 00 99 98
10 9 8 7 6 5 4 3 2 1

Library of Congress Cataloging-in-Publication Data

Blackall, Bernie, 1956-
    Basketball / Bernie Blackall.
      p. cm. -- (Top sport)
    Includes bibliographical references (p.) and index.
    Summary: Introduces the sport of basketball including its history,
  rules, equipment, and skills needed to play.
    ISBN 1-57572-632-7 (lib. bdg.)
    1. Basketball--Juvenile literature.   [1. Basketball.]   I. Title.
  II. Series: Blackall, Bernie, 1956- Top sport.
  GV885.1.B53   1998
    796.323--dc21   97-37724
                                            CIP
                                            AC

Some words are shown in **bold,** like this.
You can find out what they mean by looking
in the glossary. The glossary also helps you say
difficult words.

Contents

About basketball

Basketball is a fast, athletic, non-contact game. A basketball game involves two teams of up to 12 players each. Only five players from each team are allowed on the court at any one time. The other players are called **substitutes**.

Basketball is usually played on an indoor court with a polished wood surface. Outdoor courts are usually asphalt or concrete. The court is 94 feet long and 50 feet wide and is marked with baselines, sidelines, and a half court line, as well as a key and a free throw line (inside the circle in the key area) at each end. Teams shoot for goals at opposite ends of the court.

There is a **referee** and an umpire who control the game together from opposite sides of the court. The referee has the ultimate authority.

To start play, or to restart play after half time, the referee uses a **jump ball**, or tip-off.

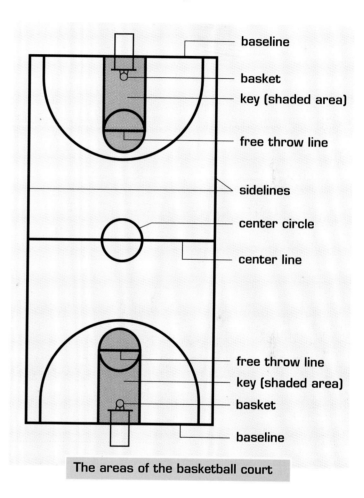

The areas of the basketball court

One player from each team stands in the center circle, facing one another, and each facing his or her own goal. The four remaining players from each team must stand outside the center circle and remain still until the ball has been tossed up.

The referee holds the ball between the two players and then throws it up into the air. The ball cannot be caught – it must be tapped. It cannot be touched until after it has reached its highest point or is on its way down.

A jump ball is also used to restart play after a **held ball** – when two opposing players both have possession of the ball. In this event, it would take place in the nearest of the three circles – the center or key areas.

U.S. highlights

In the United States, basketball has become more popular than ever. Many U.S. players are recognized worldwide. Perhaps the most well known basketball player is Michael Jordan, who plays for the Chicago Bulls. In the 1996 Olympic Games in Atlanta, both the men's and women's basketball teams won gold medals. The men's "Dream Team" was made up of the best players from the NBA. With the growing popularity of women's basketball, a new professional league has been formed—the Women's National Basketball Association (WNBA), with several of the Olympic athletes playing on different teams.

Michael Jordan—a Legend

Michael Jordan was born in 1963. He went to the University of North Carolina where he played basketball and graduated in 1984 when he was selected to play for the Chicago Bulls. He retired from basketball for personal reasons in 1993, but found he couldn't stay away and

Michael Jordan

began playing again in 1995. He is currently ranked number one in points per game in the NBA with 31.1 points per game. He was named the NBA most valuable player in 1988, 1991, 1992, and 1996. In 1996 he was selected as one of the 50 greatest basketball players in NBA history.

1996 Women's Olympic Basketball team

In the 1996 Olympics in Atlanta, the women's Olympic basketball team was undefeated and won the gold medal. They won the final competition against Brazil with a score of 111 to 97. The team included several top NCAA players. Many members of the Olympic team are now playing in the WNBA.

The 1996 Women's Olympic Basketball champions

History of basketball

Basketball, as we know it today, was invented in December 1891 by Dr. James Naismith. He saw the need for an active game that could be played indoors between the baseball and football seasons.

With just 13 rules, the original game required two goals and a soccer ball. A peach basket was nailed to the balcony at each end of the College gymnasium to form the goals. Naismith then divided his class of 18 into two teams of nine players.

His students began by passing the ball around, and then moving with the ball. They progressed to throwing the ball into the basket. A goal was worth three points. Every time a basket was made, the ball had to be retrieved from the basket using a step ladder!

The number of players was soon reduced from nine to five. To speed up play, holes were cut in the bottom of the peach baskets and backboards were added. The name of the game changed from "Naismith ball" to "basketball".

The game became popular and local competition began.

Basketball was originally played using a soccer ball and peach baskets for goals.

Basketball was an Olympic exhibition sport in 1904, 1924, and 1928. The game was first accepted as an official Olympic sport at the 1936 Olympic Games in Berlin. Twenty-two countries entered the event. The U.S. won the gold medal. Except for 1972, when they lost by only one point, the U.S.A. has won the gold medal for basketball at every Olympic Games.

What you need to play

There is one goal at each end of the basketball court. The goal ring, attached to a backboard, is suspended on a pole.

Goals

At each end of the court there is a backboard. A rim, 10 feet above the floor and 18 inches in circumference, is fixed to the backboard.

The ball

The basketball is usually made of molded rubber or leather, with a dimpled or pebbled surface. This provides a better grip for ball control. The ball should be $29\,1/2$-$30\,3/4$ inches in circumference when inflated and weigh 20-22 ounces. When dropped from shoulder height it should bounce to about waist height.

Clothing

Basketball clothing should be comfortable and loose fitting to allow for easy movement. Official team uniforms usually consist of a basketball jersey and shorts. The jersey has the player's team number printed on the front and back.

Another important item of clothing in basketball is footwear. You need well cushioned basketball sneakers to protect your feet from the impact of jumps and landings. They should also support your ankles. The soles of the boots must be non-skid. Thick socks will help prevent blisters.

Rules

The rules of basketball are designed so that the game revolves around three concepts:
- there is only incidental and non-deliberate contact between opposing players
- play flows smoothly with few interruptions and plenty of opportunities to score points
- the ball is moved around the court using the hands only

The referee can call two types of **fouls**:
- personal foul
- technical foul

Players are allowed a maximum of five fouls during a game. On the sixth foul, the player must leave the court and may no longer participate in the game.

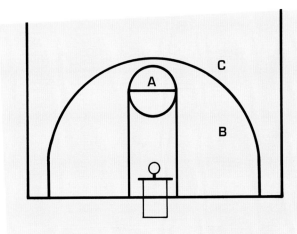

A goal will score one (A), two (B) or three (C) points depending on where the player is standing when the shot is taken.

Scoring

Each team aims to score points by shooting the ball through their goal rim. The ball must enter the rim from above. After a goal is scored, a player from the non-scoring team passes the ball from behind the baseline back into play. This is called a **throw-in**.

Points are awarded for three types of successful shots. These are:
- 3 point basket – when the player shoots from outside the three point line in general play
- 2 point basket – when the player shoots from inside the three point line in general play
- 1 point basket – when the opposition commits a foul and a **free throw** is awarded. Free throws must be taken from behind the free throw line.

Personal fouls

When you hold, trip, strike, or push another player – preventing that player from playing the ball or making a shot at the basket – a **personal foul** is called.

It is illegal for players to:
- trip or push another player
- **hold** another player's arms or body
- **block**, obstruct, or restrict an opponent's movement
- strike or **hack**
- **charge** into another player.

When a personal foul is called, the referee will point at the offending player, signal the reason for the foul and the player's number to the scorer. The opposing player is then awarded a sideline throw-in. If the player was shooting for goal and missed because of the foul, that player is given two free foul shots at goal. These are taken from the free throw line.

Each successful foul shot scores one point. On the last penalty shot, all players can compete for possession if the shot misses. If the shooter scores the basket, the non-scoring team brings the ball in from the baseline.

Body contact foul

If you run into a player who is standing still – whether you have the ball or not – you will be penalized for charging. When you are dribbling, it is up to you to change direction to avoid contact. Defenders must stand absolutely still or be moving backwards in a straight line.

Obstruction with the arm

You are not permitted to stop or slow down an opponent by extending your arm or using any other part of your body.

Obstructing another player's movement is a personal foul. This type of foul can sometimes happen when one player tries to reach across and steal the ball from another player.

A body contact foul can happen when one player tries to push into a space already occupied by another player.

Rules

Technical fouls

Unsportsmanlike behavior, which is against the spirit of the game and does not involve physical contact is called a **technical foul**. On-court players, substitutes, and coaches can be fouled for poor conduct. Technical fouls can be called for:
- unfairly distracting, insulting, or arguing with an opponent
- time wasting and delaying tactics
- jumping and grasping the rim
- unsportsmanlike behavior
- bad language

When a technical foul is called the opposing team is awarded two free shots from the free-throw line. That team's captain chooses the player who will shoot for the goal. After the free-throws, the same team also gets a throw-in at half-court.

Violations

A violation is an infringement which does not involve physical contact. There are three types of violations:
- out-of-bounds violations
- playing-the-ball violations
- time violations

After a violation the player from the non-offending team takes a throw-in from the nearest sideline.

Out-of-bounds violations

When the ball travels on or over the sidelines it becomes dead. This is an out-of-bounds violation.

If a player's foot, or part of it, is on or over the side line that player is also **out-of-bounds**. This is also an out-of-court violation.

To restart play after an out-of-bounds violation, a player from the defending team brings the ball in from the sideline.

Playing-the-ball violations

When Dr. Naismith first invented basketball, moving with the ball was an infringement. In modern basketball, players are allowed to move with the ball provided they are either dribbling or **pivoting.** Players are not allowed to kick or punch the ball, but they may roll, hit, bounce, or pass it.

Dribbling is when a player moves the ball around the court by bouncing it off the floor using just one hand at a time. The ball should be bounced once for each step. If more than one step is taken for each bounce an infringement known as **traveling** or walking with the ball is called.

Once the player stops dribbling and the ball has come to rest in one or both hands, a player may then either pivot, shoot, or pass the ball. If that player starts a second dribble, an infringement known as a double dribble is called.

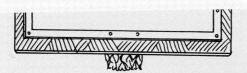

When one player takes a penalty shot the other players line up along the sides of the key. Some players will also stand nearer to the other end to wait for the ball to come back into play.

When a playing-the-ball violation is called the opposing team is given a free throw from the nearest sideline.

Time violations

During the game certain time limits apply. If you break the time limits your opponent gains possession of the ball.

The 3 second rule

When your team has possession of the ball no team member is allowed in the key area for more than three seconds at a time. Every shot at the goal is the start of a new three second count. This restriction does not apply to defenders. This rule prevents congested play in a small area of the court.

The 10 second rule

When your team has the ball, you have 10 seconds to move it across the half-court line and into your half court. Having done so, you may not return the ball to the back half of the court (the backcourt). This rule prevents stalling tactics and encourages offensive play.

The 30 second rule

Once a team gains possession of the ball the players have 30 seconds in which to take a shot at goal. This rule does not apply to junior level competition.

During each half, a coach is allowed two time-outs. The coach or player will signal to the scorer for a time-out. The clock is stopped for 60 seconds. During this time the teams may substitute players and change their tactics.

Rules

Time regulations

High school games consist of four 8-minute quarters. NBA games have four quarters of 12 minutes each. The half time interval is 10 minutes. Each time the whistle blows – for a foul or rule violation – the clock is stopped. The clock restarts when play resumes.

The team with the highest score is the winner. If the scores are even at the end of regular playing time, then an extra five minutes is played to break the tie (overtime). This continues until one team has a higher score at the end of a period.

Referee's signals

Holding

Blocking

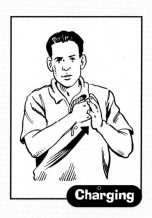
Charging

Technical foul

One free throw

Two free throws

Jump ball

Skills

Basketball involves many different skills. Practice the skills to develop and improve your play. It is important that you are competent on both your left and right sides, so practice using both hands. Good ball control will allow you to concentrate on aspects other than just the ball so you'll be able to watch your team mates and opponents. You'll also be more involved in the play and better able to make the best use of every possession.

Passing

The fastest way of moving the ball up the court is by passing it. For your team to keep possession of the ball, passes need to be accurate. If you have a choice it is generally better to pass than to dribble.

There are several types of passes. The pass you use will depend on the game situation and also the positions of your team mates and your opponents.

When you catch the ball, quickly assess your options and choose your target. Pass the ball with your hands open and fingers spread. Aim at a point between your teammate's waist and shoulders. Having released the ball, follow through with your arm toward your target.

The overhead pass is just one of the many passes used when playing basketball.

Skills

The overhead pass

The **overhead pass** is a two-handed pass used when you are closely guarded by an opponent who is shorter than you. Keep the ball over your head or slightly behind. Your wrists and forearms should generate all the power. The ball should travel in an arc, over your opponent and to your teammate.

The chest pass

The **chest pass** is a two-handed pass which is made when there is no defender between you and your target. An effective chest pass will travel in a flat line from your chest to your teammate's chest.

Chest pass
Grasp the ball with both hands, with your thumbs behind the ball and your fingers spread along the sides. Your palms should not touch the ball.

Step forward with your knees bent and push the ball using your fingers. Flick your wrists forward as you release the ball.

Overhead pass

Hold the ball above your head or slightly behind. Your fingers and thumbs should be spread behind the ball.

Keep the ball above your head as you step forward into the throw. Flick your wrists to push the ball forward.

Push pass

With the passing hand behind the ball and your fingers spread, choose your target. Your free hand helps to balance the ball. As you step forward push the ball from your shoulder line.

The push pass

The **push pass** is a single-handed pass used over a short or medium distance.

An effective push pass should travel in a flat, straight line to your teammate.

Skills

The baseball pass

The **baseball pass** is a single-handed pass, similar to the way a baseball catcher would throw the ball.

It has a short wind up and an explosive release.

Baseball pass

Bring the ball back behind your ear with your fingers spread behind the ball. Your weight should be on your back foot. Step onto your front foot as your arm and then your wrist propel the ball forward. Follow through with your hand towards your target.

The bounce pass

When you are being guarded by a tall opponent, or if your opponent's arms are raised, you can **bounce pass** the ball. You pass the ball under rather than over your opponent.

The ball is pushed to the floor with a single bounce before it reaches your team mate. The ball should travel about two thirds of the way between you and your target before it bounces. It should reach your teammate at between knee and waist height.

Receiving passes

After working so hard to get possession, it is vital that your team keeps the ball. Whenever a pass is executed it must be accurate. The ball should always be caught cleanly. The receiver should watch the ball rather than the player who is passing it. The receiver's hands should be held high or low – depending on the pass – ready to receive the ball.

When receiving it is important to always:
- keep your eye on the ball
- move into an open space away from your opponent
- give your team mate a target by indicating with your hand where you want to receive the ball
- receive the ball with both hands, with your fingers spread around the ball

Skills

Ball handling

Dribbling is the most basic ball handling skill in basketball. Dribbling is bouncing the ball continuously, while moving or standing still, without letting it come to rest in one or both hands.

Your wrist and fingers control the ball when dribbling. Your palms are not used. Only one hand is allowed to have contact with the ball at any time, but you can change hands as often as you wish.

Whether attacking or defending, players tend to gather close to one another at either end of the court. To avoid crashing into your opponents, for which you would be fouled, you need to be able to stop quickly. There are two types of techniques used to stop: the jump stop and the stride stop.

A jump stop is when you stop by landing with both feet together, as you would for a jump. A stride stop is when you stop with one foot in front of the other foot.

Once you have stopped, using either technique, you can receive the ball or **pivot**.

Dribbling
Push the ball down firmly with your forearm, wrist and fingers. The ball should bounce at least as high as your knees but not higher than your waist. With slightly bent knees, and your weight on the balls of your feet, keep the ball in front and to the side of your body.

Shooting

A basketball game is won by the team that scores the most points – and you can only score by shooting the ball through the basket. Good goal shooting is a vital skill, one that every team member should be competent at.

The type of shot you take will depend on the situation. If you are within shooting range and are standing still, you will usually take a **set shot** or a **jump shot**.

A **lay-up** is the logical shot when you are dribbling towards the basket.

Grip

Adopt the same grip for each of the shots. Spread your fingers behind the ball – your palm should not touch it at all. Your non-shooting hand balances and guides the ball from the side. Keep the ball above and in front of your head with your shooting hand on your shooting side.

Dribbling allows you to move around the court with the ball.

Pivoting

When players receive the ball, or when they come to a stop after dribbling, they are allowed to change the direction they are facing by pivoting. When pivoting, one foot (the pivot foot) must remain on the same spot without leaving the ground. The other foot may lift off the ground to move. Players are allowed to pivot in any direction. Pivot on the ball of your foot.

If the pivoting foot is moved while that player still has the ball, a playing-the-ball violation is called.

When shooting a basket, the palm of your hand should not touch the ball.

Skills

The set shot

The set shot is the easiest shot. It is used when an opponent is between you and the goal.

The jump shot

The jump shot is similar to the set shot, and the most often used. Instead of just straightening your legs, you jump from one spot, or you dribble the ball as you run into the shot and jump to release the ball from the highest point of the jump. Because it is released from a higher platform, it is a shot that is very difficult to defend.

Jump shot

Dribble the ball as you approach the goal. Plant both feet firmly and bend your knees. Point your shooting elbow directly at the goal.

Use your legs to push yourself up as high as you can. Take the ball high and release it just as you reach the highest point of your jump. The ball should travel in a smooth arc. It should be on its downward flight as it hits the backboard or rim.

Set shot

Stand still with your knees slightly bent. Your shooting hand should be behind and slightly under the ball. Your fingers should be spread.

Point your shooting elbow at the goal and bring the ball down towards your shoulder. Bend your knees further.

Push up with your legs and body and extend your arms, hands and fingers. Release the ball near the peak of your lift, flicking your wrists and fingers.

Skills

The lay-up

The lay-up is used when you are on the move as you dribble close to the goal.

Aim the ball at the nearest top corner of the rectangle on the backboard behind the basket. Guide the ball upwards and aim for it to rebound into the basket.

The slam dunk

Only players with exceptional spring and skill can perform a slam dunk. It requires the player to leap high enough to dunk the ball into the basket from above the rim with either one or both hands.

Rebounding

When a shot for goal is missed the players jump to **rebound** the ball.

When in defense you aim to win possession of the ball off the rebound. If you are unable to win it cleanly (grab the ball outright), tap it away from your opponents.

Lay-up
As you approach the goal, gather the ball with both hands to begin the shooting action. Look up at the basket as your foot comes forward to land. This will be your take off foot. The shooting action starts by lifting the ball up in front of you with both hands.

Players need to be tall to slam dunk a basketball. Many professional basketballers will slam dunk.

When playing in offense (when you are attacking), and a shot for goal fails, try to tap and push the ball up for another attempt at scoring. If you are able to take the ball cleanly, pass it to a teammate and move quickly out of the key area.

Drive your knee (the knee on the same side as your shooting hand) up to give you extra lift. Your shooting hand should be behind and slightly under the ball with your fingers spread and pointing upwards. You should be airborne and at full stretch as you release the ball.

Defense

When playing defense your team must prevent your opponents from getting into a scoring position. Many tactics can be used either by individual players or by the whole team.

When your opponent has the ball, use your hands to prevent them from passing. Your palms should face your opponent and your knees and body should be bent. Be ready to move quickly to the left or right, forwards or backwards.

Defensive skills are important in a game. Remember that an opponent under pressure – which is the case during a game – is more likely to make a mistake. This is your opportunity to take possession of the ball.

Man-to-man defense

Man-to-man defense is when one defending player guards one offensive player. When playing man-to-man defense your main objective is to stay between your opponent and the basket. This usually prevents your opponent from shooting for goal and, therefore, forces them to pass. You should:
* adopt a defensive stance
* shuffle your feet sideways
* move in the same direction as your opponent
* form a flat triangle

To form a flat triangle, stand with your back to the basket, about a step back from your opponent with the ball. You should be between your opponent with the ball and that player's teammate who is waiting to receive the ball. You should have your hands out in front, ready to intercept the pass. You are aiming to block your opponent and stop him or her from passing the ball.

The defensive stance.

Zone defense

When playing **zone defense** each player is responsible for defending a specific zone. When individual players defend their zones effectively, it forces the opposing team to take long range shots which are less likely to score.

Defending against a dribbler

As your opponent dribbles towards the goal you need to move in the same direction. With a defensive-type stance, move to a position between your opponent and the basket. Keep moving with the play and stay between your opponent and the goal. Only move your feet and legs, maintaining your defensive hand, arm and upper body position. If an opportunity arises, intercept and steal the ball.

When you are defending against a dribbler, you should move in the same direction as your opponent.

To form a flat triangle, stand with your back to the goal, with one hand pointing at the ball and the other hand pointing at the opponent waiting to receive the ball.

Getting ready

It is important to stretch and warm up before exercising or playing sports. Warming up will make you more flexible and your muscles and joints will loosen up. This helps to prevent injuries. Do some light/slow movment before starting. Stretching cold muscles can cause injury.

Hamstring stretch
Sit on the floor with one leg stretched out straight in front of you and the other leg bent so that your foot touches your knee. Reach forward and touch your toes. Hold the stretch for 30 seconds. Repeat on the other side.

Arm stretch
Bend and lift your arm behind your head. Push your elbow back with your other hand until you feel the stretch.

Bench jump
Stand sideways next to the bench. Jump sideways up and onto the bench and down to the other side. As you become more confident you can jump from one side to the other without stopping on the bench in between. Jump from one side to the other 10 times. This should only be done when you are thoroughly warmed up.

Ball dribble

Move and dribble the ball for 3 minutes. Change hands and direction throughout the exercise.

Bent knee sit-ups

Lay flat on your back with your knees bent and feet on the floor. Holding a basketball in your hands, use your stomach muscles to lift yourself up towards your knees. As you sit up the ball should be straight out in front of you. Do this 10 times.

Neck stretch

Stand upright and place your hand on the other side of your head. Gently pull your head sideways until you feel the stretch. Repeat the same stretch on the other side.

Chest passes

Chest pass to another person, or against a wall, 20 times.

Thigh stretch

Bend one leg behind you and pull in up with your hand. You might need to hold onto another person or lean against a wall for balance. Hold the stretch for 20 seconds. Repeat on the other side.

Taking it further

Basketball Associations

Naismith Memorial Basketball Hall of Fame (NMBHF)
1150 W. Columbus Ave.
PO Box 179
Springfield, MA 01101
☎ (413) 781-6500

National Basketball Association (NBA)
645 5th Ave. 10th Fl.
New York, NY 10022
☎ (212) 826-7000

Women's National Basketball Association (WNBA)
645 5th Ave.
New York, NY 10022
☎ (212) 688-9622

More Books to Read

Allen, J. *Basketball, Play Like a Pro*. Mahwah, NJ, Troll Communications L.L.C., 1997

Basketball. New York, Chelsea House Publishers, 1997

Morrison, Lillian (comp). *Slam Dunk*. New York, Hyperion Books for Children/Hyperion Paperbacks for Children, 1997

Silverman, B. *Superstars of Women's Basketball*. New York, Chelsea House Publishers, 1997

Glossary

baseball pass a single-handed pass similar to a throw a baseball player might use

block to stop the progress of another player by blocking their path

bounce pass a pass which bounces once before reaching its target

charge to deliberately or accidentally run into another player

chest pass basic flat pass used over medium distance

defense when the opposing team is in possession of the ball your team is playing in defense

free throw a penalty shot taken after a foul, from behind the free-throw line

hack when a defending player slaps or hits an opposing player in an attempt to stop a shot for goal

held ball when two opposing players both have their hands firmly on the ball

hold to stop another player's movement by holding them

jump ball is when the ball is thrown high up into the air between two players; used to start and restart play, also called tip-off.

jump shot shooting for goal from a jumping position jumping off two feet

lay-up a shot for goal while you are airborne and moving towards the goal jumping off one foot very close to the goal.

man-to-man defense when one defending player marks an attacking player

offense when your team is in possession of the ball and is trying to score goals

out of bounds the area outside the court –includes the lines, back of the backboard and the supports

overhead pass a two-handed pass over the head of your opponent

personal foul a foul involving personal contact with an opponent

pivoting rotating on one foot without lifting that foot off the ground

push pass a short one-handed pass from shoulder height

rebound when the ball bounces off the ring or the backboard after an unsuccessful shot

referee an official who controls the game and upholds the rules

set shot a free throw shot, or a 2 point shot from the field

substitutes reserve players who come on to replace teammates

technical foul any poor conduct that does not involve physical contact

throw-in passing the ball from the boundary line to an on-court player after a rule infringement

travel moving illegally with the ball also called walking.

zone defense each defender guards an area of the court

Index